The Forbidden Room

Alan Gorevan

Copyright © 2020 by Alan Gorevan

ISBN: 9798634014289

THE FORBIDDEN ROOM

CHAPTER ONE

Caroline Doherty sat in her little Peugeot, staring out the side window at the hills of west Cork. The air in the car was icy, but not as cold as outside. She gripped her phone, hoping the device would pick up a signal for the first time in half an hour.

This remote corner of Ireland was famous for its rugged beauty. Its hills, valleys and peninsulas were spectacular, not to mention its jagged cliffs towering over the Atlantic Ocean.

Caroline and her boyfriend, Jason Murphy, were headed for The Cliff View Guest House, located on the Beara Peninsula in the extreme south-west of the country. Evening was falling and the hotel was still some distance away. They were in a hilly area. Nothing but grass and rock all around them.

It was a terrible place for a car to break down.

As far as Caroline could tell, the nearest town was ten or fifteen miles away. Getting there would demand a long, dangerous walk. As well as being twisty, the road ahead was narrow and, of course, had no footpath.

The road behind them was equally bad. She couldn't imagine walking back to the petrol station they'd stopped at a few miles earlier. Out here, each mile felt like ten.

The late February light was beginning to fade. If they were walking on the road and a car came along, they'd be almost invisible. Jason was wearing a puffy black coat and dark jeans. Caroline's jeans and olive-coloured jacket were almost as dark. Her blonde hair was the only thing that might be visible in the gloom. Still, she figured that a driver was more likely to knock them down than give them a lift.

The road had clearly been cut out of the hillside, and there was not an inch to spare on either side. A rocky cliff rose up on the right side while, on the left, a hill of gorse fell away sharply. Rocky hills filled the middle distance.

Caroline opened the car door. At once, she felt the pounding of the rain. She opened her umbrella and walked over to Jason, who was still fiddling with the engine. Caroline was certain he had no more idea than she did about what was wrong with it. He insisted on trying to fix the thing anyway.

"Any luck?" Caroline shouted to be heard over the rain.

"Not yet."

Valentine's Day was meant to be romantic. A weekend break in the wilderness. Though they were both from Cork City, Caroline had taken frequent trips into the wilderness of West Cork when she was growing up. This place was a different world.

Largely unspoilt, it possessed a rough beauty that Jason didn't seem to appreciate. He was always more interested in staying in the city, or even going to Dublin, rather than exploring his own county's wild side.

"Can you shine a light here?" Jason shouted. He was bent over the engine, his face almost touching it.

Caroline turned on the torch on her phone and pointed it where Jason's hands were making a fumbling, uncertain exploration. It reminded her of the first time he'd tried to unhook her bra.

"It'll be dark soon," Caroline said.

"Why do you think I want a light?"

"I mean, we need to do something."

Jason straightened up and turned to her. His long black hair was plastered to his face and neck. His features, normally so chiselled and handsome, twisted into a sneer.

"What do you want me to do? I'm trying to start the fucking car."

Caroline flinched. During their six months together, she had rarely seen him angry. He hadn't wanted to come here, she knew. He'd only agreed to please her. But she'd been sure he'd start to enjoy himself once he arrived. She couldn't have known the car would cut out in the middle of nowhere.

"Look," she said, "I can't get a signal. You can't fix the car. We should try walking."

Jason looked around.

"On these roads?"

"I know, but we can't stay here. We have to try something," Caroline said. "We have to go somewhere."

"Just let me fix the car, will you?"

"You've been at it for ten minutes."

"If you weren't nagging me, I'd be finished by now."

Nagging.

The word slapped her across the face. So she was a nag now. Her first serious boyfriend had said it. Jason turned his attention to the engine again, not seeming to notice how much his words had hurt her.

Caroline turned off the torch app.

"Hey," Jason said, but she ignored him, and walked towards the back of the Peugeot. She didn't want to sit in the car. It was stopped in the middle of the road, blocking the lane. She imagined another car coming along and smashing into them. It was unlikely – traffic out here was infrequent – but her stomach churned with dread all the same.

She went and got the red warning triangle from the car's boot. She walked forty paces from the back of the car and set the triangle down on the tarmac. The only reason she hadn't put it out earlier was that Jason had seemed so confident he'd have the car running again in no time.

Just a second – that was the phrase he'd used, after the car cut out.

Caroline shook her head, wondering why she had listened. Jason played bass guitar in a rock band. He hadn't a mechanical bone in his body.

Just a second could mean *all night*.

As she was walking back towards the car, a gust of wind got under the umbrella and tore it from her hands. She let out a shout of surprise, and watched the umbrella fly away, over the side of the road and down the hill. She hurried over and looked down after it. An almost vertical drop greeted her. The ground levelled off far below, maybe eighty feet down. Nothing but gorse and rock and yellow heather. And – what was that?

Caroline squinted, shielding her eyes from the rain.

Was that…?

A flash of light on the road distracted her. She turned to see headlights approaching.

"Someone's coming," she shouted.

Caroline had never been so happy at the sight of a stranger's car. She'd started to get worried. After all, it was dark and stormy, and they were broken down, with no way to contact anyone. She jogged back to the Peugeot.

"What did you say?"

She grabbed Jason by the arm. "I said, someone's coming."

He straightened up. "I've nearly got it figured out," he said. "I think what we have here is a bad actuator."

"Never mind that. There's a car coming."

Ignoring Jason's scowl, she turned on her phone's torch function again and went around the side of the Peugeot. Standing in the middle of the other lane, she waved her hands in the air. The car was coming from the direction they had come. Maybe they could get a lift to The Cliff View Guest House.

The headlights of the oncoming car grew larger. It didn't slow.

"Can they see us?" Caroline asked. She waved her phone higher in the air, hoping the light would be obvious.

The car was nearly upon them, and its roaring engine made Caroline's chest tighten. She waved her arms and called out, "Hey. Hey."

Jason straightened up and looked at the approaching car. His eyes widened.

"It's not stopping," he said. "Get out of the way."

CHAPTER TWO

Liam McGlynn's pale fingers shook as he gripped the steering wheel. The teenager was driving too fast. The truth was, he shouldn't have been driving at all – not in his state, and not in this weather.

Liam had driven halfway to his girlfriend, Emily's, house before he changed his mind and pulled in at the side of the road. He stopped there, intending to give himself a little time to think things over, but instead his eyes welled up with tears, and he sobbed like a child.

He wanted to get away from there. To be far away, with Emily by his side. But involving her in this was selfish. Liam had no money. He had nothing. Asking Emily to go away with him would have been asking her to give up any chance of a decent life. Liam didn't want that.

So he'd wiped his eyes with the sleeve of his hoodie, turned the Range Rover around and started to drive back home. He didn't want to do that, but what other option was there? No one was going to help him. No one cared.

As he approached the local petrol station, Liam saw an unfamiliar grey car at the pump. A seven-year old Peugeot 5008. Diesel. Manual transmission. It was pointed west, so he figured the driver was heading towards Liam's house.

He pulled in at the side of the forecourt and watched a couple get out of the car and head into the shop. They looked to be in their twenties. A skinny guy with long black hair, curled like it belonged to an 80s rock star, and a blonde woman, just as thin. They both wore puffy jackets and tight jeans. They looked like relatively normal people.

Liam got an idea.

He stepped out of the Range Rover. Crouching low, he hurried over to the Peugeot and grabbed a handful of sandy gravel from the ground. Liam knew engines. With a mechanic for a father, they had been a part of his life since he was born. He figured his idea might work.

He opened the fuel cap and shoved the gravel into the tank.

A second handful, then a third.

What he was planning was dangerous – and not just for him – but he could think of no other way out.

Liam glanced inside the shop. The woman was paying for her purchases. He closed the cap and, keeping low, jogged back to the Range Rover. When the couple emerged from the shop, he lowered himself in his seat so they wouldn't see him.

They probably wouldn't have observed him anyway. They were so absorbed in each other, talking and laughing. It was like the way he and Emily were, during their rare moments together.

Liam heard the couple drive off. He was relieved that their car was able to start. If it hadn't, then his plan would have failed. He rose in his seat, his heart thumping like crazy. Too shaky to drive.

It was fifteen minutes before he was calm enough to follow.

There was no sign of them on the road. He wondered if the gravel would do the job. It ought to, but when? The road ahead was empty.

Had he put enough gravel in?

What if it didn't work?

His stomach churned with anxiety, and he felt that he was going to be sick.

But when he rounded the next corner, he saw them. Dead ahead, the Peugeot's hazard lights were flashing. He drove through the red warning triangle almost before he registered its presence.

Despite the cold, his hands were slick with sweat. He wiped them on his hoodie, one after the other. The lady stood in his path, waving her arms.

I can't stop, Liam thought. *No way.*

He hit the accelerator.

CHAPTER THREE

The car veered into the wrong lane, hurtling towards Caroline. Its headlights were huge, blinding. She was still waving her hands in the air when she realised that it was going to hit her. To smash right into her without stopping.

She now saw that it was a huge, black SUV, the perfect vehicle for this terrain. The roar of its engine filled Caroline's ears. It was moving too fast, almost upon her. The driver pressed on the horn but didn't slow.

Caroline turned, trying to get out of the path of the danger, but her movements seemed sluggish. Her chest felt tight. This must be how a deer felt when it was blinded by a car.

I'll never make it, Caroline thought. *I'm going to die.*

The observation was terrifying, but at the same time, it felt strangely detached. Suddenly she felt light-headed. Caroline knew she was the one who was in danger, but it was as if she was watching someone else struggle to get to safety.

Then Jason grabbed her.

He pulled her towards him. Even as she was moving towards him, it was with excruciating slowness.

The car was almost upon her. She could smell its fumes.

Caroline squeezed her eyes shut and braced for the impact.

She felt heard the roar of the SUV's engine, felt its vibration in her chest, and then the vehicle shot past.

Caroline and Jason fell to the ground next to the Peugeot's front bumper. Jason hit the tarmac first, his head smashing against the ground, and Caroline fell on top of him, his body cushioning her fall. Jason grunted as the air was squeezed out of his lungs.

Caroline's heart was hammering in her chest.

She was alive.

"Are you okay?" she said.

"Yeah." Jason exhaled slowly. "You?"

"I think so."

Breathing hard, she disentangled herself from him. They staggered to their feet. The SUV disappeared out of sight around the corner. Jason came and stood next to Caroline.

"Maniac," he shouted.

Caroline shook her head. "What was that about?"

"They were going to drive straight into you."

Caroline shuddered. Her legs were weak as jelly. The rain continued to hammer down hard. "I don't understand how someone could act like that."

"Did you see the driver?"

"No. Not with those headlights in my eyes. I couldn't see a thing."

Jason glanced at the darkening sky. "I guess we shouldn't stand around here."

"Now you agree that we should walk?"

"Do you want an argument?"

"No," Caroline said.

"Your hands are cut," Jason said.

Caroline nodded impatiently. "You know, I saw something, before that car came." She walked to the edge of the road and looked down the steep hillside. Jason followed her.

"What?" he said. "I don't see anything."

Caroline shivered. Both of them were drenched to the skin. The puffy jacket she wore was sold as "water resistant" but that was a lie. The rain had started soaking into it as soon as the first drop hit the fabric. Her eyes scanned the land below.

Caroline pointed and said, "Look down there."

"At the bottom?"

"Yeah. See that grey line? Is that a road?"

Jason squinted for a long time. "It's hard to tell, with those bushes in the way. No," he said at last. "I don't think so."

"I think it is."

"Why did you ask me then?"

She ignored him. "There might be a house," Caroline said. "It looks like a one-lane road. Private property."

Jason looked sceptical. "Even if it is, how are we meant to get there? We might have to drive miles to find the way to it. And the car is still dead."

"A straight line is the shortest distance between two points," Caroline said. Though the hillside was very steep, Caroline figured they could scramble down it if they were careful. She played basketball once a week and went to the gym at least twice. She wasn't afraid of a little exertion.

"Are you sure?" Jason asked. "I don't want you slipping and breaking your neck."

"Like you say, if we go the long way around, it could take hours. If we go this way, it might take a couple of minutes. Let's go."

Jason looked reluctant, probably because the plan wasn't his. He'd probably have preferred to continue tinkering with the Peugeot's engine.

"Hold on."

He ran back to the car. Opening the back door, he took out their overnight bags, then jogged back over.

He said, "Better to bring them, right?"

"Sure. Can you help me down?"

Jason placed their bags at his feet and held onto Caroline's hand as she lowered herself from the side of the road to the grassy slope below, a gap of three or four feet.

Jason jumped down next to her, but he lost his balance, got caught in the two overnight bags, and rolled into some bright yellow heather. He got to his feet, swearing loudly.

"Watch out," Caroline said.

"Fuck off."

Maybe it was the fact that she had nearly died, but Caroline felt a touch of giddiness. Relief at being alive. She grabbed Jason's neck, pulled his face close to hers, and kissed his cheek.

"I love you," she said.

Jason stared at her. Neither of them had said those words. And just a few minutes ago, Caroline had felt like killing him.

But whatever.

She was *alive*. That was worth celebrating.

Smiling to herself, she set off down the slope, being careful to keep her balance as she stepped on rock and mud. Heather brushed against her legs. The valley floor was not a long way down, but she hated even moderate heights.

Over the rain, Jason shouted, "Someone should build a slide here."

Caroline smiled. "That would be fun."

"Did you recognise the SUV?"

"No. Why would I?"

Jason said, "I think I saw one like that at the place where we stopped."

Caroline thought back to the petrol station where they bought a snack. She had been completely focused on selecting chocolate bars while Jason chose a packet of crisps. Sweet versus savoury. They never agreed on anything. She didn't remember any other customers.

Caroline shrugged, "I don't know. Maybe."

They continued down. After a minute, Caroline reached the place where her umbrella had landed after being blown out of her hands. It was caught up in more heather. She worked it free and closed the umbrella. There was no point trying to shield herself from the rain now. They were as wet as they could get, and Caroline needed both hands to keep her balance. She stuffed the umbrella into the pocket of her jacket and continued on her way.

They finally reached the bottom of the hill. A rough road stretched out in both directions.

Caroline nodded to the left. "I think it's that way."

"How do you know?"

"A feeling."

She didn't wait for a reply, just started walking. The trail curved around a rocky outcrop and led downwards.

"We're probably going the wrong way," Jason grumbled.

The road went on much longer than Caroline expected. They walked for ten minutes before a huge yew tree appeared ahead of them.

"Do you hear that?" Jason said.

"What?"

He said, "Sounds like the sea."

"I don't hear anything." *Except rain,* Caroline thought.

"You're not a musician. Your ears aren't trained like mine."

Caroline walked around the yew tree.

Standing in front of her was a large, ramshackle bungalow, its stonework covered in peeling white paint.

Lights blazed in its windows.

CHAPTER FOUR

In the sprawling garage, Liam McGlynn stepped out of the Range Rover. He closed the door and walked to the house, zipping up his hoodie, and then his jacket, to protect himself from the bitter cold.

It was a miracle he hadn't crashed on the way home as he wasn't in control of himself. He kept thinking back to earlier in the day, remembering the sound of the mirror breaking.

Stop it.

There was a way out.

The couple in the Peugeot had broken down at a good place, but that didn't mean they'd find the house. Liam hoped they would, though. There was nothing else nearby.

The panicked feeling he'd had since lunchtime had only grown worse as the Range Rover bounced along the road to the house. Terror snaked up Liam's throat as he wondered what Doreen and Steve would do.

For Liam, it had always been *Doreen and Steve*, never *Mum and Dad*. They didn't let him use those words. Only Frank had been allowed to say that.

What if they discovered the trick he'd pulled with the couple? They were already at his throat.

Liam was starting to regret not going to Emily's house as he had planned. Perhaps the two of them didn't need to run away. Maybe her parents would shelter him. Liam could have explained things – could have *tried*, anyway. Emily was sympathetic.

Some people shouldn't be allowed to be parents.

She said that after Liam told her about the goldfish.

Doreen had purchased them when Liam and Frank were eight. One fish ate the other while the boys were at school. Liam had cried when he found out – because it was his fish that had been eaten. Doreen said it didn't matter. His fish was only a poor copy of its brother.

"Like you," she added.

Nearly a decade later, Liam still felt a chill when he remembered the way Doreen looked at him as she said it.

He walked around the back of the bungalow, rubbing his hands together as he went.

Steve stood outside the door with a cigarette in his hand. He gave Liam a cool stare as his son approached. Liam stopped, well away from him, and put his hands in his pockets.

"Where did you go?" Steve said.

"For a drive."

"Who'd you talk to?"

Liam shook his head. "Nobody."

They were both silent for a minute. Steve took a puff on his cigarette and pointed towards the sea.

"Barney went sniffing down the cliff face. You better find him before dark."

Liam's heart sank. His golden retriever wasn't a smart dog, and he hoped it hadn't got too near the cliff edge. A rough path ran parallel to the sea for the best part of a mile and was a favourite place of Barney's. But he shouldn't be wandering there during a storm, not as evening set in.

"I'll look for him," Liam said.

He turned and set off across the grass separating the paved area around the house from the cliff two hundred paces away. The wind howled and pushed Liam back as if it wanted to stop him going.

He had only made it a couple of paces before Steve caught up, grabbed Liam by the neck and pulled him close.

"You think things will just go on? You think it doesn't matter?"

Liam struggled to break free.

"Let me go," he shouted.

"It should have been you," Steve hissed in his ear.

Liam reached into his jacket pocket, where he always kept an LED torch, about three inches long and one inch in diameter. It came in useful when you lived in the middle of nowhere, with no street lighting. His fingers closed around it as Steve gripped his neck tighter.

"By the way," Steve said, "you are one ungrateful—"

Liam pulled out the torch and smashed it as hard as he could into Steve's face. With a grunt, Steve released him and fell in a heap on the ground.

Liam ran towards the cliff before Steve could recover.

CHAPTER FIVE

The sight of a house out here would have been startling enough, but behind it the land fell away in a dramatic cliff. It was as if some enormous monster had taken a bite out of the land. Caroline stared, hypnotised by the churning waves of the Atlantic Ocean.

She turned her attention to the bungalow, a large building shaped like an L, with the middle of the L pointing at the sea. Caroline didn't care how it looked. She only wanted to get inside. She started forwards.

"Wait a minute," Jason said. "What if this is where the driver lives? The person who nearly drove into us?"

"Good. I want to give him a piece of my mind."

"Him?" Jason squinted at her. "You're so sure it's a man?"

Caroline sighed. "Maybe you want to stand in the rain all day arguing, but I'd like to get indoors."

"I'm just saying, we don't know who lives here."

"Then let's find out."

She left Jason standing there and walked towards the house. A large garage stood to the side of the bungalow. Its double doors were closed.

Caroline made her way up to the door. It was solid wood. No glass in it, so she couldn't see inside. No sign of a doorbell. She knocked – knocked hard, to be heard over the rain. As her knuckles rapped on the wood, Caroline heard voices inside. They fell silent as soon as she knocked.

She glanced at Jason, as he caught up with her on the doorstep.

"Did you hear that?"

Jason nodded. "Let's go," he said. "I don't like this."

"We can't go now. They heard us."

"I don't want to walk in on… you know."

Jason hated family disagreements, even mild ones. His parents had split up when he was thirteen. Jason rented his own flat the day he turned eighteen and hadn't spoken to his family in the seven years since.

Caroline touched his arm.

"We'll ask to use their phone. We'll call for help. That's it. It'll take ten minutes. Then we can get on with our weekend."

Jason looked at his watch. "It's five o'clock now. I'm not feeling very romantic."

"Neither am I," Caroline said, "but I planned this whole weekend for you."

Jason sighed. "Fine."

Caroline tried to cheer herself up. The Cliff View Guest House was waiting for them. It would have sparkling wine and a bowl of fruit ready at check-in, plus a vase of fresh flowers in the bedroom. She had chosen a room with a breath-taking view of the Atlantic, nothing but waves as far as the eye could see, though she was getting a preview of that vista now, and the sea looked rough.

A hiking tour of the cliffs was arranged for the following morning. She'd thought it would be something to look forward to, after spending this evening enjoying local seafood and relaxing in the bar.

Booking the weekend had made Caroline feel like an adult. At twenty-seven, she considered herself a late bloomer. She had never gone away with a boyfriend before, had never even had a serious boyfriend before. Jason seemed special.

Now, as she watched a vein bulge in Jason's forehead, Caroline wasn't so sure about that.

He said, "Jesus, are these bastards going to open up or not?"

He pounded his fist against the door.

"Hello? Anyone home?"

Caroline heard footsteps approaching.

CHAPTER SIX

Steve McGlynn staggered towards the house, his hands out in front of him as if he was blind, though he wasn't. He was just dazed.

Shielding his eyes from the rain, he glanced back at the path that ran along the cliff face. Liam had already vanished into the darkness.

"You'll be back," he shouted.

Steve touched the side of his head, beside his eyebrow. His fingers came away bloody. He wondered how bad the wound was. It hurt like a bitch. For a second, he'd thought the little prick was going to kill him.

Kill *him*.

After everything Steve had done for him.

The back door of the house swung open and Doreen poked her head out. Steve's wife hadn't changed much since they met nearly thirty years earlier. She'd been a top-of-the-class veterinary student. He'd been an apprentice mechanic. Steve knew the moment he saw her that there was something special about Doreen. He hadn't changed his mind about that.

When angry, she still gave him that look, her deep-set eyes burning darkly, but her face otherwise blank.

She took in at a glance his injury and the fact that he was alone.

"Where's Liam?" Doreen asked.

Still dizzy, Frank reached out and grabbed the handrail next to the door. Doreen took his arm and helped him into the kitchen, closing the door behind her.

"Gone," Steve said. "Ran off to find Barney, once he smashed me in the face."

Doreen helped him to a chair at the kitchen table and said, "We're not going to let him away with it."

Steve shook his head. "I don't intend to. But he's strong as a horse, that boy." His eyes narrowed. "What exactly should we do?"

Doreen had always been the one with a plan. When they met, she'd been so determined to become a vet. Of course, she hadn't been allowed to finish her degree after her dean found out she'd been the one killing the squirrels on campus. Hard to understand the fuss. Damn things were only rodents. Maybe Doreen shouldn't have hung them around the campus from tree branches though.

She said, "We have to punish him. Did he talk to anyone?"

"I don't think so."

"If he opens his big mouth, who knows what he might say?"

Steve scowled. "We didn't do anything wrong. He's the one who—"

Someone knocked on the front door. The sound was so unfamiliar, it took Steve a moment to recognise the sound.

"Did you hear that?" he said.

Doreen opened the door to the hall.

Someone pounded on the door again. A man's voice. "Hello? Anyone home?"

Steve's eyes widened. "Oh shit," he said. "They're here to arrest us."

"Shut up," Doreen hissed.

"Don't open the door," Steve said. "They'll go away."

"The lights are on."

"They'll go away," he repeated.

"We can't act suspicious. You go and get yourself tidied up," Doreen said.

"Don't," Steve said. "You'll make things worse."

But Doreen was already walking down the hall.

CHAPTER SEVEN

Caroline waited as the door opened to reveal a stout woman in her fifties. She wore an apron over a flowery blouse, and beige trousers. Curly, greying hair framed a round face, but something about her mouth reminded Caroline of a trout.

The woman kept her hand on the door, as if ready to slam it shut again if they gave her a reason.

Caroline's nostrils filled with the smell of baking. Something sweet and fruity. Her stomach rumbled.

Jesus, are these bastards going to open up or not?

Jason's words rang in her ears. Caroline couldn't remember the last time she'd been so mortified. Why did he have to say such a thing?

"We're so sorry to bother you," Caroline said. She smiled at the lady. "Our car broke down on the road."

She pointed back the way they had come.

"Broke down?"

"We don't know what the problem is but—"

"Maybe a bad actuator," Jason interrupted.

The woman stared at their soaking clothes.

Caroline said, "We weren't able to call a mechanic. My phone couldn't find a signal. Could we use yours to call for help? We'd really appreciate it."

The woman seemed to think for a moment, then opened the door wide.

"You better come in," she said, stepping back.

Caroline smiled. "Thank you so much."

She wiped her feet on the welcome mat inside the door. The woman closed the door behind Jason. Narrow as it was, the hallway was warm, and for that Caroline was grateful. The dark blue walls were covered with framed photos of a family.

"This is a lovely house," Caroline said. It was only a white lie.

"Thank you," the woman said. "Follow me."

She had a stronger Cork accent than Caroline or Jason, maybe because they were from the city. This woman's accent was so strong, it turned *follow me* into a question, and had a musical, lilting quality.

Caroline glanced at the photos as she followed the woman down the hall. They showed the woman at various ages, always with a man and a boy. No, two boys. But one liked to lurk in the background.

"Sorry for dripping water on your floor," Caroline said.

"Don't worry about it."

That sounded like a question too.

The woman closed the door to a laundry room. Not the prettiest room in the house, Caroline guessed. She glimpsed a washer, a dryer, and a rack with keys on the wall. Of course, the woman wasn't expecting guests. How would Caroline have felt if two strangers turned up on her door without any warning and she had to let them in? She'd be wondering what to hide too.

The woman led them into a sprawling kitchen. It was even warmer in here, and the scent of baking was stronger. Caroline's mouth watered. If she had seen a photo of this room in a magazine, the kitchen would have been described as rustic. It had an old wood-burning stove, tins and glass jars everywhere. No sign of a microwave or anything else modern.

Through the window, Caroline could just about discern the movement of the ocean. The thought of its cold, dark water made her shiver.

A groan made Caroline whip around. There was another doorway on the other side of the kitchen.

"Don't worry," the woman said. She took off her apron and put it on a hook next to the oven. "That's only my husband. He slipped in the garden."

"Is he hurt?" Caroline asked. "I did a first aid course at work."

"He's fine. Don't worry. I'm Doreen McGlynn, by the way."

"I'm Caroline. This is Jason."

They shook hands. Doreen's grip was firm. There was a firmness in her blue eyes, too.

"Is it just you and your husband here?" Jason asked.

Doreen's eyes twinkled. "Oh no. We have the twins. Frank and Liam."

Caroline caught sight of a landline on the wall.

"Can we call somebody? I'm happy to pay you."

Doreen shook her head. "I wouldn't take your money, even if the phone worked. But the line is down."

"Pardon?" Jason said.

"The storm has knocked out the line. You can't phone anyone."

CHAPTER EIGHT

Caroline's disappointment must have registered on her face because Doreen reached out and squeezed her arm. Caroline didn't like strangers touching her, but she was too surprised to protest.

"It's okay," Doreen said. "The phone will be working again soon."

"You mean tonight?" Jason asked.

"Oh, no. The storm is getting worse. Look at that." Outside, the rain had turned to sleety snow. It slapped against the window, and began to pile up on the sill. "No one's going to be out fixing things tonight."

"Fuck," Jason said. "This is unbelievable."

Caroline shot him a look. "Jason."

"Excuse me," he said. "But fuck."

Doreen lumbered over to the window and closed the curtains.

Caroline pictured herself and Jason trudging back to the car, getting inside the ice-cold interior and freezing to death during the night – if they weren't rear-ended by another motorist first.

Jason said, "Is there no mobile phone signal around here?"

"It's always hopeless," Doreen said. "You have to go a few miles down the road to get a reliable signal."

Jason shook his head in disbelief. "How do you live here?"

"Well, it has its good points. There's the peace and quiet. And usually we're in communication with the world. Oh, my baking!"

Doreen opened the oven, and used a pair of mitts to remove a tart with rich golden-brown pastry. While she set it down on the worktop, Caroline closed the oven door.

"Thank you," Doreen said, giving her a smile.

"So," Caroline said. "There's no way to contact anyone tonight?"

"I'm afraid not," Doreen said, straightening up. "The good news is my husband's a mechanic. I'm sure he'd be happy to look at your car."

"Excellent," Jason said.

"But he can't do it tonight. Not in this weather, and not with the bang on the noggin he just got. But in the morning." Doreen glanced at Caroline again, then looked Jason up and down. "We have a spare room. You're welcome to stay the night with us."

"That's very kind, but we don't want to impose. You don't even know us."

"I don't think there's much of a choice. Look at you. You're drenched. And it's snowing now." Doreen leaned forward. "You'd die out there."

Jason ran a hand through his hair, a reliable indicator that he was frustrated.

"You're very kind," Caroline said. "I guess we'll have to take you up on that offer."

Doreen waved her hand. "Living in the countryside makes you practical. You do whatever you have to do."

Caroline heard footsteps. A moment later, the door to the kitchen opened and a man Doreen's age appeared. He was stout, a little more so than his wife, and had a kiwi-fruit haircut and a short, grey beard. He wore round glasses with golden frames.

Caroline stared at the gash on the side of his head.

She said, "Oh my god, I think you need stitches."

The man glanced at Doreen. She walked over and put her arm around him.

"Say hello to Caroline and Jason. Their car broke down on the road. I've said they can wait here till morning. This is my husband, Steve."

"That's rotten luck," Steve said, sounding genuinely upset.

Doreen led her husband to a chair at the kitchen table. He lowered himself into it slowly. When he put a finger to his head, Doreen slapped it away.

She said, "I'll fix up Steve's wound and then we'll see about getting you two warm and dry."

"Thank you so much," Caroline said. "There's no hurry."

Water was dripping from her hair down her face. Despite what she said, she could feel the cold and wet seeping into her bones. The woman was right. They wouldn't last long outdoors tonight.

CHAPTER NINE

Caroline began to feel her clothes drying off in the heat of the kitchen. Doreen had given her and Jason towels to dry their hair with, and that helped.

Steve sat at the kitchen table, with Jason next to him. Caroline hovered nearby, hoping to make herself useful, as Doreen cleaned out Steve's wound with a damp cloth.

"Looks like you need some TLC too," Doreen said, when she noticed Caroline's grazed palms.

"Sorry?"

"Tender loving care. You better rinse those cuts."

"Oh, right."

Caroline washed her hands under the cold tap. As she dabbed them dry with a few sheets of kitchen roll, she told Doreen how she had been forced to jump out of the path of the SUV.

Doreen dabbed antiseptic onto a tissue and patted Caroline's wounds. It stung. Caroline winced but didn't make a sound.

"A black SUV?" Doreen said thoughtfully.

"Do you know anyone who owns a car like that?" Caroline said. "A neighbour of yours, maybe?"

Doreen shook her head. "We don't have a lot of neighbours around here. Four-wheel drives are common, but I don't know anyone with a black one. And I certainly don't know anyone who'd drive like that."

Jason piped up. "That bastard would have driven straight into Caroline. I swear I'll kill him if I ever find out who did it."

Caroline cringed, wishing Jason would shut his mouth. His obnoxious comments might get them kicked out of the house.

Doreen opened a large first aid kit in the middle of the table. She had an impressive variety of gear.

"Are you a doctor?" Caroline asked.

"Close enough," Doreen said. "Studied to be a vet, though I never qualified. I don't throw anything away. You never know when something will come in handy."

She sterilised a needle, scissors and a pair of tissue forceps. She even had a packet of nylon suture material.

"This stuff has a high tensile strength," Doreen said.

Jason looked away as she started to stitch Steve's wound shut. Doreen's tongue stuck out between her lips while she concentrated on her task. It was an oddly girlish gesture in a woman of her age.

I hope I live to fifty, Caroline thought.

She shuddered at the thought of her lucky escape, how close she had come to being killed before she even turned thirty.

Blood dripped down Steve's face as his wife worked. He seemed calm, or else he was still dazed from his fall. Either way, he didn't protest.

Jason kept his eyes averted. Though he came across as a tough guy, Caroline knew he couldn't stomach the sight of blood. He didn't like to talk about it much, but Caroline had gathered, over their time together, that Jason's father was a violent drunk. Hence the broken marriage. And hence the broken bones that still gave Jason grief if he played bass guitar for too long at a time.

"There," Doreen said, finishing up. She dabbed the wound and admired her handiwork. "You sit down and have a rest."

Steve grunted as he got to his feet. He adjusted his glasses, then padded off towards the front of the house.

Doreen turned to Caroline.

"Now. What should we do with you two?"

CHAPTER TEN

Doreen left Jason and Caroline in the kitchen and went to make up the spare bedroom. Caroline had offered to help, but Doreen wouldn't hear of it, and Caroline could understand that. She might not want her guests to see the spare room yet, if it was a mess.

"Now don't touch my apple tart," Doreen said, waving a finger at them.

She clicked the door shut behind her.

"These people give me the creeps," Jason said. He jumped up from the kitchen table and walked in a circle around the room. "There's something wrong with them."

"Shut up. There's something wrong with *you*."

"I'm serious."

Caroline rolled her eyes. "Because they live in the countryside?"

"Yes," Jason said. He rubbed his eyes. "No. But living in the countryside doesn't help. It's not a point in their favour – I'll tell you that much."

"They're giving us a room for the night. They're taking us in."

"I wouldn't do that if I was them."

"Because you're so selfish."

Jason reversed his direction and began circling the room the opposite way.

"Exactly," he said. "Normal people are selfish."

"So you're saying this sweet couple has some sort of ulterior motive? That's why they offered to let us stay here?"

"Maybe."

"Like what?" Caroline said.

Jason shrugged. He stopped pacing and stood in front of the apple tart.

"I'm so hungry," he said.

"Oh my god." Caroline watched as Jason reached out. "Don't even think of touching that," she hissed.

"I want to try it."

"Don't."

Jason shot her a wolfish grin and thrust his index finger into the tart. He pulled it out straight away.

"Fuck!" he shouted. "It's hot."

Caroline hissed, "Of course, it is. Be quiet."

He put his finger in his mouth and sucked it.

"Jesus."

He went to the sink and put his finger under the cold-water tap. When he took it out from under the water, his finger looked as pink as a crab.

"Nice going," Caroline said.

"Tasty, though."

A gruff voice said, "What's going on?"

Steve was standing in the doorway.

"Sorry," Caroline said.

"What was that shouting?"

"I sat on my finger," Jason said.

"Sat on your finger?" Steve frowned.

"Sorry," Caroline said. "We'll keep it down. How are you feeling?"

"Fine. A little dizzy."

"Maybe you need to sit down?"

"Yeah. You're probably right."

Steve turned and left the room.

Caroline breathed a sigh of relief. Jason could be so goofy sometimes. The apple tart sat on the worktop, a big finger-hole in it.

"That's great," she said. "That's just great. They ask us not to do one thing, and you do it."

Jason grinned. "What are they going to do about it?"

CHAPTER ELEVEN

Fifteen minutes later, Doreen led Caroline and Jason down a hallway. The house had a weird layout with the kitchen at centre, the point where two hallways met. Doreen pushed open the door to the spare bedroom.

"I made up a bed for you and tidied the room a little."

"Thank you so much," Caroline said. She stepped inside and saw a double bed. Doreen had left some towels on top of the covers. A wardrobe stood on one side of the bed and a computer desk on the other.

Doreen said, "There's only one bed. Do you mind sharing?"

"Not a problem," Jason said.

Doreen took a pile of clothes off the desk and set it down on the bed.

"I found you some dry clothes. My old stuff for you, Caroline. Some of Frank's for you, Jason. That's our eldest son."

"Great," Jason said. "Because our bags are soaked through. We can't wear any of our spare clothes."

"Don't worry. I'll do the laundry tonight. Wash and dry all your clothes. In the meantime, I hope Frank's clothes fit you. The bathroom is at the end of the hall. You can have a shower and get warm."

Caroline smiled. She felt genuinely touched by the woman's kindness.

Doreen stepped back into the hallway.

"Get nice and warm and dry," she said. "Then come and we'll see about dinner. It'll be ready in half an hour. I hope you have a good appetite."

Caroline smiled. "Oh yes."

"You didn't spoil it?"

"Nope," Jason said.

"Good. Make yourselves at home."

Caroline said, "Again, thank you so much."

She followed Doreen out to the hallway. Doreen smiled and turned to go back towards the kitchen. Caroline walked down the hall, stopped at the next door, and reached for the handle.

"Not that room!" Doreen shouted.

Caroline pulled her hand back in shock. The woman was glaring at her.

"I'm sorry. I—"

"The bathroom is at the end of the hall. The end!"

"Sorry. I don't know what I was thinking."

Caroline felt like a school pupil being scolded by a belligerent teacher. Jason appeared in the doorway of the spare room, a confused look on his face. Doreen walked over to Caroline.

"It's okay," Doreen said. "But that's Frank's room. Don't go in there. He's very private, very particular about his personal space. Enjoy the rest of the house. Relax in the kitchen or the sitting room. Whatever you like. But not Frank's room."

"I'm so sorry," Caroline said.

"The bathroom is at the end of the hall. Okay?"

"Absolutely. Got it. We won't bother Frank." Caroline gave a nervous laugh. She stopped smiling when Doreen didn't smile back. "Where *are* your sons?"

"Oh, they're around somewhere."

"Will they be joining us for dinner?"

"I'm sure they will. Liam will, at least. I better let you get cleaned up."

Doreen turned and walked away.

Caroline felt shocked by Doreen's reaction. She followed Jason into the spare room.

"Was that weird or what?" he said.

Caroline was breathing too hard to reply for a moment. Her body reacted to emotional stress as if it was physical exercise. "A bit," she finally managed to say.

Jason was examining the spare clothes Doreen had left him.

"Not my style," he said, looking at the woolly cream-coloured jumper. He unfolded the pale blue jeans. "Not my style."

"I'll have a shower," Caroline said, because she thought if she didn't get a break from Jason, she'd slap him.

Doreen had left her a pair of baggy jeans, a T-shirt and a warm jumper. They were far too big, but Caroline didn't mind, as long as she got into something dry. There were socks too, but no underwear.

"Are we going commando?" Jason said.

"I guess. I'm drenched all the way through."

Jason nodded thoughtfully and went over to the window. He pulled open the curtains and looked out into the darkness of the evening. Sleety snow was still falling.

He said, "Why do I feel creeped out?"

"How would I know? Because you're an over-sensitive musician?"

"Let's just get out of here as fast as we can, okay?"

Caroline was surprised when Jason turned, and she saw his face. He wasn't goofing around like he had been in the kitchen.

"Okay," she said. "Shower, eat, sleep. Leave first thing in the morning."

Jason nodded. "Sounds like a plan. Though I'd still prefer to leave right now."

"Go ahead."

He smiled. "Maybe I will."

CHAPTER TWELVE

Liam McGlynn jogged along the cliff path, hood up, gloves on, his chest burning. The sleet had stopped for the moment, but an icy wind continued to gust.

The slate grey sea churned a hundred and fifty feet below. It was at times like this that the immensity of the ocean impressed itself upon Liam. Salty sea air filled his senses.

The path was only a few paces from the cliff edge. Sometimes Liam was tempted to hurl himself over the edge. It would be a brutal fall. The cliffs were rocky and you could easily hit the cliffside as you fell. Then at the bottom, your body would be broken on the jagged rocks where the waves crashed.

No, he had a job to do.

He had to find Barney. No one else cared about the golden retriever, but Liam loved that dog. Barney was out here somewhere, alone. Liam couldn't stand the thought.

Moving quickly, he urged himself down the path. He thought of Emily. Liam could hardly believe he'd found a girl who wanted to spend time with him, someone who cared. But he had. Emily and Barney. The only things in the world that he cared about.

Tonight was no ordinary night. He'd get away from this hellhole. Tonight. He promised himself he would, just as soon as Barney was safe.

The thundering roar of the waves was fantastic. Liam wondered if he'd be able to hear Barney if he barked. He continued jogging for another ten minutes but found no sign of the dog.

What if Barney had returned to the house?

It seemed likely, given the weather.

Liam decided to turn back. But before he did, he shouted his dog's name. The wind tore his voice away. He waited but there was no response, no sign of Barney anywhere.

CHAPTER THIRTEEN

Caroline left Jason pondering his fashion choices in the bedroom. She took the towels and Doreen's spare clothes and stepped into the hallway.

Six doors opened onto the hall. One led back to the kitchen. There was the guest room that she and Jason had been assigned, and another door stood opposite. It was slightly ajar, and Caroline glimpsed a bedroom. The décor looked mature, so she figured the room belonged to Doreen and Steve.

She started down the hall, passing Frank's room on the way – the room she was forbidden to enter. She wondered why Frank was so private. What did he do in there? There was no sound from within, so Caroline thought Frank must not be home.

A fifth door faced Frank's room. Maybe this one belonged to the other son, Liam. No sound from that room either.

At the end of the hall was the sixth and final door.

The bathroom.

Caroline stepped inside. The room was bigger than she expected, nothing like the cramped one she had in her own apartment. Everything here was blue, from the tiles on the walls to the ceramic sink, and even the toilet bowl. It looked weird and somehow dated. But it seemed clean – except for a spatter of blood on the mirror.

Steve must have come here to check his wound.

The bathroom was a little cooler than the rest of the house.

The window had no blind, but its glass was heavily frosted, so no one could see in – at least, they could see nothing more than a blur – which was a relief, considering that she was on the ground floor.

She closed the door behind her and reached down to lock it, only to find that there was no key in the lock. There was no bolt either, no way to secure the door.

As far as Caroline was concerned, a lock was the number one thing you needed in a bathroom. Maybe they didn't have many guests out here, but still, four people lived in the house. How could they not want to lock the door?

"Okay," she said.

It was what it was.

She should just get on with things.

Be fast.

She used the toilet quickly, watching the door the whole time, and listening for the sound of someone coming. Nothing, except the sound of the wind outside.

She set down Doreen's spare clothes on top of a small chest of drawers, then stripped. She piled her own wet clothes on the floor.

Now that she was naked, she felt vulnerable. She opened the glass doors of the shower stall and peered at the electric shower. The machine looked simple enough, not like the baffling devices in most hotels. Reaching in, she turned on the water, and adjusted the temperature until it was as hot as she could stand. Then she stepped under the water and closed the doors behind her.

Relief washed over her and she began to warm up under the falling water. There was shampoo and shower gel on the shelf in the shower stall. They had a pleasant floral scent, and Caroline enjoyed the luxurious feeling the hot shower gave her.

She decided to leave Doreen and Steve some money as compensation for using their bathroom supplies. Caroline didn't have a lot of cash, but she wasn't stingy with what she did have, and she felt guilty for imposing on them – especially if Steve was going to help them tow the Peugeot in the morning.

She turned off the water and stepped onto the towel on the floor.

The air felt different. Thinner. Caroline looked around, confused.

The door to the hall stood open an inch.

Caroline stared at it. She had shut the door. Even though she hadn't been able to lock it, she'd shut it firmly. She didn't see how it could have opened by itself. Had someone come into the bathroom while she had been showering? While she had her eyes closed?

47

No.

Surely not.

She crossed the room quickly and closed the door. She pulled the handle to see if it opened easily, but it didn't.

Maybe Jason was messing with her? He could be annoying. But would he be this mean?

Caroline noticed that the pile of wet clothes was gone. Only a small puddle of water remained.

Someone *had* been in the room.

She went over to the pile of clothes she had set down on the chest of drawers, intending to get dressed as quickly as possible.

Someone had placed a pair of lacy underwear on top of the pile.

CHAPTER FOURTEEN

Once she had dressed, Caroline hurried down the corridor to the bedroom. Doreen's old jeans were so loose at the waist, Caroline had to hold them up as she walked.

She had left the underwear in the bathroom. She wasn't going to wear them. For one thing, they belonged to someone else, or they had at one time. The thought of wearing another woman's panties disgusted her. For another thing, she was livid at their appearance in the room.

How dare someone invade her privacy like that?

She pushed open the door to the spare bedroom and stepped inside.

"You're never going to believe this…" Caroline said, but the room was empty. Where was Jason?

She ducked back into the hall, then made her way to the kitchen. Doreen was standing at the oven. A teenage boy stood next to the door to the back garden. He had messy brown hair and skin that was pale as milk. He wore a fluffy black hoodie over a purple T-shirt, plus pale jeans and runners. The boy looked nervous.

Caroline remember being that age. Sometimes she wondered how she'd ever got through it. And how people had tolerated her.

Coming into the room, she had fully intended to demand to know who came into the bathroom while she was showering. The sight of the boy's face changed her mind. He looked like he'd just been slapped across the face with a fish. Was it him? Did he put the underwear in the room as some kind of joke? Or maybe Doreen was the one who had entered the bathroom, and she was just trying to be helpful.

Caroline decided to hold off on making any accusations.

"This is my son, Liam," Doreen said.

Holding the jeans with one hand, to keep them from falling down, Caroline went over and held out the other out to Liam. He swallowed – she saw his Adam's apple move – and then gave her a limp hand. Caroline took it and did all the shaking.

"Nice to meet you."

The boy muttered something she didn't catch.

Caroline said, "Where's Jason?"

"Outside, smoking with Steve." Doreen shook her head. "Sometimes, I really don't understand men."

Caroline nodded. "It's a filthy habit."

"I smoke too," Doreen said. "But not outside during a blizzard."

"Oh, well," Caroline said, "each to their own."

The top half of the back door was glass, covered by a blind. Caroline lifted it and peered into the darkness. It was fully dark now and she couldn't see anything.

She sighed.

"I suppose your husband definitely wouldn't be able to tow my car tonight?"

"I don't think so. He's still woozy. He really shouldn't. And don't worry, there'll be no traffic on the road tonight. No one's going to hit your car."

"That's what I'm worried about."

"No need," Doreen said. "I promise."

Caroline turned to Liam. "Do you drive?"

"I, uh—"

"He's only seventeen," Doreen said. "He's still learning. Don't you worry. Everything is going to be fine." She took a step closer to Caroline and pinched her cheek. "You're so… *conscientious*."

Caroline forced a laugh, but the pinch hurt.

"Casserole's ready," Doreen said. "Let's eat. If we can round up the men."

CHAPTER FIFTEEN

Steve and Jason walked around the bungalow while they smoked. Jason hadn't had a cigarette since Christmas, and it felt so good.

He had decided against a shower. While Caroline was in the bathroom, Jason had changed out of his wet clothes and put on Frank's dry ones. When he went to the kitchen, Steve was getting a beer from the fridge. Would have been rude to refuse. And cigarettes went so well with beer.

From the back, he could see how large the house was. It looked like it had been added to over the years, giving the building a ramshackle quality.

"The previous owner was a builder," Steve said, pointing his cigarette at the house as they walked.

Not a good one, Jason thought, but he said nothing.

His hands were numb, but he savoured the nicotine rush.

"What do you do out here?" Jason said.

Steve broke out in a fit of coughing. "Enjoy the peace," he said. "We like to keep to ourselves most of the time. I do auto repairs. Doreen is a natural born baker. Sells her cooking at a farmer's market and online."

"That must be tough when the internet isn't working."

"It works most days."

There was no moon. Though Jason could sense the immensity of the ocean nearby, he could see little.

They walked around the side of the house, to where the garage stood.

"Are you going to show me your tow truck?" Jason said.

"Not right now." Steve threw his cigarette on the ground. "We better get back inside. I reckon dinner is ready."

"Just a quick look? I'm pretty curious. I always wanted to drive one of those things."

Jason heard the kitchen door open.

"Dinner," Doreen called.

Steve smiled in the darkness. "Let's go. You don't want to make her wait. She can be mean as hell."

CHAPTER SIXTEEN

Doreen removed the casserole from the oven. She instructed everyone to sit down at the table while she plated the meal.

Liam helped, bringing plates to the table. He was relieved Caroline and Jason had found the house. Their presence meant he was safe for the moment.

He could see that the rich smell of the food stirred them, the scorching hot tomato sauce with onions, pork chops and beans. Whatever else Doreen may have been, she was a skilled cook, who could make anything delicious.

Liam sat down next to Jason, across the table from Caroline. She smiled at him.

"Did you find your dog?" she asked.

Liam shook his head. He'd found no trace of Barney. Nothing on the cliff path, no sign Barney had returned to the house.

"I'll look again later," Liam said.

Caroline nodded.

"I'm sure he's fine. Dogs are smart. They always find their way home."

Liam said nothing. He needed to speak to Caroline and Jason. Urgent as it was, he knew he'd have to wait until later. He couldn't say anything with Steve and Doreen watching.

"Thank you for this meal," Caroline said, looking at her plate. "This smells wonderful."

"There's nothing like home cooking," Doreen said, handing Jason his plate. Who wants a drink?"

Jason said, "I'll take another beer."

"Caroline?"

"Just water for me, please."

Steve got the drinks. Then he and Doreen sat down at the table and everyone began to eat.

"This is wonderful," Caroline said after the first bite. "Scrumptious."

"Thank you."

"Nice painting," Caroline said, noticing a watercolour on the wall behind Liam. He didn't need to turn around to know which one she was talking about. The picture of the bungalow had hung on the wall for years.

Jason turned and looked at it.

"Huh," he said. "It's the same as the one on *that* wall."

Now it was Caroline's turn to look behind her, to where Jason was pointing. Another picture. Same composition, same colours, same bungalow. She said, "Are they identical?"

Doreen waved a warning finger at Caroline. "Be careful. You'll start Steve off on his favourite topic."

"What's that?"

"I painted one of them," Steve said. "The other is a copy. Can you tell which is which?"

Jason put down his fork and walked over to the picture behind him. "This is a real painting," he said. He walked over to other one, examining that too. "But so is this. They're both originals."

"Interesting way of looking at it," Steve said. He put a forkful of casserole in his mouth and waited until Jason sat down again before he continued. "I painted one in a burst of inspiration. A few weeks later, I copied it as precisely as I could."

Jason nodded. "So they're both originals, as I said."

"I wouldn't put it like that," Steve replied. "With the first one, I was excited. I was inspired. When I did the second one, I felt nothing. I was just copying."

"But you painted them both," Jason insisted. "You got a brush and applied paint onto a canvas?"

Steve leaned forward in his seat. "Let me ask you a question. Do you believe things have an essence?"

"What do you mean?"

"It's, you know, hard to define… something that sets one thing apart from another."

Jason frowned. "I don't follow."

"Like the difference between an original Van Gogh and a photocopy. They're completely different, right?"

Jason's lips curled into a sneer. "Sure. The original is worth twenty million euro. A copy might be worth ten."

He took a long drink of beer.

"Right." Steve said. "Why is that?"

Jason shrugged. "One is the real deal."

"But what *makes* it the real deal? It's the same picture. Looks the same on the wall, right? Shows the same thing. Uses the same colours. Why is one worth so much and one worth so little? Most people wouldn't be able to tell them apart if their lives depended on it."

"I'm not sure," Jason said slowly. "One was painted by a genius. The other was printed by a machine."

"So what?"

"So," Jason said, "one is real."

"What does that *mean*?"

Doreen took Steve's arm. "I'm sure these nice young people couldn't care less about your views on art."

Caroline smiled. "The question is interesting. It's about what you think the thing is, rather than what the thing actually is."

"Bullshit," Jason said, draining his beer bottle.

"I agree with Caroline," Doreen said. "Take a different example. This dinner, say. Do you like the pork?"

Jason nodded. His plate was almost empty, so clearly he was enjoying it.

"Absolutely delicious," Caroline said.

"Now what if I told you it isn't pork? What if I told you it was Barney, Liam's dog?"

Liam froze.

"What?" Jason said.

"What if I killed his dog and used its meat in the casserole? Would you feel differently about what you're eating?"

Jason said, "That would be disgusting."

"Why?" Doreen said. "You've been enjoying it up to now. Who cares if it's pig meat or dog meat? Maybe they taste the same. The only thing that's changed is your *idea* of what you're eating. Just like Caroline said."

Caroline laughed. "What an example."

"Sorry," Doreen said. "Bad illustration. I don't want to put you off your food. I used pork, by the way. Swear to god."

She laughed, then forked some casserole into her mouth. The others continued eating too, after taking a moment to put the image out of their minds.

But Liam couldn't.

His stomach was doing cartwheels. He fought the urge to vomit, but it was hard because he was sure what Doreen had said really was true. Barney was dead, and they were eating him. It was part of Liam's punishment.

Doreen gave him a nudge in the ribs.

"Eat up," she said.

CHAPTER SEVENTEEN

Caroline swallowed her last bite of casserole. Dinner had been delicious, though Doreen's joke about dog meat had been in bad taste, and almost put Caroline off it. She drained her glass of water and glanced at Jason, who was finishing his third beer.

I hope he doesn't drink any more, she thought.

Jason couldn't handle it. After a couple of drinks, he got surly, then sleepy, and finally, maudlin.

Steve cleared the empty plates away. Caroline tried to help him, but he shooed her away.

"Sit down, sit down," he said with a smile.

"Thank you, Steve. How's your head?"

"Much better."

Doreen stood up. "Who wants dessert?"

"I'd love some," Caroline said. She still had a little room left. Always did when it came to sweet things. Sugar was her weakness. "What is it?"

"Apple tart with ice cream."

Caroline swallowed, remembering the way Jason had stabbed his finger into the tart earlier.

"Lovely," Caroline said. She forced a smile.

"I'll take some too," Jason said.

"You want a beer with that?" Steve said. "Or maybe something stronger?"

"Sure."

"Both?" Steve laughed and headed over to the fridge. "Let's have a beer first. We can move onto the heavy stuff later. Nothing else to do."

Doreen brought the tart over and set it down in the middle of the table. The gaping hole in the pastry screamed at Caroline. It couldn't have been more obvious. Doreen and Steve would be furious with them for ruining dessert. She was surprised that Doreen hadn't said anything yet. Caroline braced herself for the coming rebuke.

Doreen got a long, sharp-looking knife.

Caroline glanced at Jason.

Will he apologise? No, he never does.

She didn't know whether to say something. She decided to wait and see what happened.

Doreen began to slice the tart, cutting it into six equal slices.

"Are you saving a slice for your other son?" Caroline asked.

"Of course," Doreen said. She glanced at Liam. "We can't forget about Frank."

"Where is he?"

"Visiting friends."

"I guess he won't be home tonight. I mean, with the weather being what it is."

Doreen nodded but said nothing. The knife sliced through the tart, right next to Jason's finger hole.

She must see it, Caroline thought. *She sees it, but she's too kind to mention it.*

Doreen put an intact piece of tart on Caroline's plate.

Caroline wanted to say thanks, but her throat was dry. Now the knife was slicing through the tart on the other side of the finger hole. Another intact slice went onto a plate for Jason. Doreen cut three more slices and plated them.

Finally, only one slice was left. The one for Frank. The one that Jason ruined.

It sat in the middle of the table, untouched, while they ate in dead silence.

CHAPTER EIGHTEEN

After dinner, Steve made tea for Caroline. It was not a brand Caroline liked but she wasn't going to complain. At least it warmed her.

Steve and Doreen drank bitter-smelling coffee. When Steve had finished his, he stood up and slapped Jason on the shoulder.

"Come to the sitting room," he said. "I have a nice bottle of whiskey I've been waiting to crack open. Might as well do it today."

"Now you're talking," Jason said.

He gave Caroline a shrug before disappearing down the hall.

Doreen began tidying up the dishes, piling them up by the sink. Liam sat sullenly at the kitchen table.

Caroline hated feeling useless, especially now that she was a guest in someone else's home. She didn't think she could look at the ruined slice of apple tart for another minute. She got to her feet.

"I'll wash the dishes," she said. "It's the least I can do."

"No need," Doreen replied. "It's Liam's turn. He'll do it."

"I can help, then."

"No. Liam will handle it. Won't you?"

The boy nodded. "Sure," he said.

Caroline wondered if he was feeling alright. His voice sounded thin, and his face was paler than it had been earlier.

"Caroline, you just take it easy," Doreen said. "I have some wine, if you'd like a glass?"

"No, thanks. I don't usually drink alcohol."

Doreen stared at her as if she'd never heard of such a thing before. "Oh?"

"I like to keep a clear head."

"Sensible." Doreen nodded slowly.

"You know what? I think I'll go to bed if that's alright with you," Caroline said.

"So early?"

"I'm a little tired. I'll try to catch some sleep. About our clothes—"

"They're already in the washing machine. Don't worry about a thing. In the morning, everything will be clean and dry, and Steve can help you with your car."

"Wonderful. I don't know how to thank you."

"Don't worry about it," Doreen said.

Caroline gave a little wave. "Well, good night."

"Night."

Caroline went to the bedroom. Her overnight bag was gone. Had it been in the room after her shower? Caroline couldn't remember. She was only sure that it had been wet. Maybe Doreen had put it in the washing machine too.

Caroline found her toilet bag on the dresser. She took it with her and went to the bathroom. The lacy underwear sat where she'd left them. Caroline shuddered. She had forgotten about them.

Everything over the last few hours seemed like a kind of dream. The first part had been exciting – driving through the natural beauty of the Cork landscape with her boyfriend, looking forward to the fun ahead. Valentine's Day in a nice hotel. The second part was more like a nightmare – the breakdown and the maniac driver in the SUV. At least, they had found the McGlynn house, though.

They were lucky.

Caroline brushed her teeth and went back to the bedroom. She turned on the bedside lamp.

A sheet of white paper, folded once, sat on top of her pillow. Caroline opened it and read the message scrawled in pen.

I need help. PLEASE DON'T TELL Steve and Doreen. Meet me outside at midnight.

CHAPTER NINETEEN

Once he'd left the note on Caroline's pillow, Liam hurried down the hall to the kitchen, wiping his sweaty hands on his T-shirt as he went.

He was gambling everything on a stranger's help. He had no choice. But if Caroline said anything to Steve or Doreen about the note... well, Liam didn't want to think about that.

He opened the door to the kitchen to find Doreen staring at him.

"Where were you?" she said.

"The toilet."

"Finish the dishes."

She sat at her usual chair at the kitchen table.

Liam wanted to ask about Barney, wanted Doreen to confirm his worst fear, that she had killed the dog to punish him, put its meat in a casserole and made him eat it. He desperately wanted to know for sure that his dog was not lost in the storm.

But he wasn't going to ask. Experience had taught him that Doreen would never tell him the truth. Instead, she'd draw out the agony and uncertainty for as long as possible, teasing and tormenting him.

He made his way to the sink and began washing the dishes.

"Make those plates clean enough to eat off," Doreen said. Her favourite joke.

Liam supposed he was seven when he started to wonder if his mother was evil. With his father, it happened a little later.

He remembered the magic trick Steve performed for Frank and him on their seventh birthday. Steve called it 'the duplicator'. He'd rigged up a bunch of old engine parts to look like a piece of fancy scientific equipment, and placed it in the sitting room. He also set up a curtain rail, with two red curtains. The curtains hid an area on each side of the machine.

Frank and Liam sat on the couch, eagerly waiting for the magic show to begin.

"Are you ready, boys?" Steve asked.

"Yeah," they shouted.

"I bought you a present, son." Steve was talking to Frank. He held up a goldfish bowl.

"Can I feed it?" Frank asked.

"Later. Right now I'm going to use this little guy to perform some magic."

Being the younger twin by a whole nine minutes, Liam never got the good presents, the good food, the hugs and kisses.

Steve made a big show of putting the goldfish bowl behind one of the red curtains, jiggling with his scientific 'apparatus', and announcing that the duplication had been successful. He pulled back the curtain on his right side, showing them Frank's goldfish again. He then revealed, with a flourish, what was behind the red curtain on the other side of the machine.

"Ta da," Steve said. He pulled back the curtain to show another goldfish in another bowl.

"There we are. An identical copy."

The boys looked at it in amazement, fully believing that he had really made a copy of the fish appear out of nowhere.

"Is it the same fish?" a grinning Steve asked the twins. He handed Frank the first fish bowl, then held up the second one for them both to examine.

"No," Frank said, squinting at the fish suspiciously.

"What do you think, Liam?"

"I'm not sure."

Frank punched him on the arm. "Who cares what he thinks? He's a copy too. He's just a copy of me."

Grinning, Steve handed Liam the second fish. "For you. A copy for a copy."

Liam might still have been haunted by that day, even if that was the only trick. But Steve hadn't finished with them yet.

"Let's duplicate something else," he said.

The twins went silent as they waited to hear what he would choose to copy next. That was when Doreen walked into the room. Immediately, Liam felt uncomfortable, like something terrible was going to happen.

"No," he said. "Don't."

Doreen back-handed him across the mouth. He fell back in the couch, too stunned to cry. When he sat up, his mother was stepping behind the curtain and his father was starting 'the duplicator' again. It began making noise, while Steve made a show of fiddling with the dials and switches.

Then the machine fell silent.

Steve watched the two boys' faces as he whipped away the red curtain to show their mother still standing where she had been before. Then he reached over the other side of the machine and pulled away the curtain there – to reveal another woman. She had Doreen's fleshy face and deep-set eyes, and she was dressed in the same cardigan and cotton pants.

"Hello boys," she said.

Even her voice was the same.

An identical copy of their mother.

Thinking of it now, as Liam washed the dishes in the kitchen, tears welled up in his eyes. It must have been awfully easy to fool a couple of kids, who had never been told that their mother had a twin sister.

Liam didn't learn the truth until that evening, when he overheard the sisters laughing about it over wine.

Yeah.

That was when he decided Doreen wasn't just mean.

She was evil.

CHAPTER TWENTY

Caroline sat on the bed and read the note again.

I need help. PLEASE DON'T TELL Steve and Doreen. Meet me outside at midnight.

Clearly the message had been written by Liam, but Caroline didn't know what to make of it. Was it a joke? Based on what Caroline had seen of the teenager, he didn't seem like the joking kind. If anything, he came across as depressed and anxious, like so many teenagers.

Like Caroline used to be.

There had been times as a teenager when she desperately felt the need to reach out to someone, even a stranger. Someone she thought would understand her. Was that what Liam was doing? Maybe he wanted to tell her something that he thought his parents wouldn't understand.

But why outside? Why at midnight?

The wind gusted against the window, moving the curtains slightly. She felt the breeze on her face. Single-glazed windows, out here? Amazing.

She put the sheet of paper on the nightstand and took off her jumper. Then she got under the duvet, still wearing Doreen's jeans and a T-shirt. Caroline was reluctant to take off the jeans, even in bed, since she wore nothing underneath. Not very comfortable, but she figured she could tolerate it for one night.

Her phone said it was nine thirty, still early. She left the lamp on and lay there, thinking this wasn't how her Valentine's Day was meant to turn out.

Caroline heard a door open in the hallway.

Her breathing quickened. She told herself not to be so silly. There was no reason to be scared. All the same, she reached out and turned off the bedside light. As footsteps approached her door, she pulled the duvet up to her chin.

The footsteps stopped outside her door.

Caroline held her breath. The handle began to move. Someone was coming in. Was it Liam? Perhaps he had decided he couldn't wait until midnight, and needed to speak to her now.

The door began to open.

Light from the hallway hit the wall beside the bed.

The door didn't creak, but Caroline heard the faint sound of its movement as it opened wider. The silhouette of a man appeared on the wall.

The man standing in the doorway.

Liam? Steve?

She swallowed. Waited.

"Caroline?"

She sat up at the sound of the whisper. "Jason?"

Flicking on the bedside light, she saw her boyfriend standing in the doorway. He smiled. "You okay?"

"Come in," she said. "Close the door."

He did. "What's up?"

"Nothing."

Jason looked half-drunk. She decided not to tell him about the note. If Liam's message was sincere, then they couldn't tell Doreen and Steve about it. But Jason, when he was drunk, was unable to keep a secret. Caroline couldn't trust him to keep the note to himself.

He came over to the bed and sat next to Caroline. She could smell the alcohol on his breath.

"Aren't you coming to bed?" she said.

"It's not even ten yet."

"I know, but what is there to do out here?"

"Exactly," Jason said. "There's nothing to do. The TV isn't working. The internet isn't working. We're just talking. Steve's telling funny stories."

"And you're getting drunk."

"We had a couple of glasses of whiskey."

"Is that a good idea? Why don't you come to bed?"

"Soon," Jason said. "Don't nag."

"Fine."

She turned away from him. Felt a flash of irritation when he put a hand on her hip.

Caroline said, "Don't even think about it."

"What did I do?"

"I'm not in the mood."

"Fine. Whatever," Jason said. "I thought it was Valentine's Day."

He stood up and left the room, closing the door behind him.

Caroline set the alarm on her phone for 23:50, then closed her eyes. She figured Jason was one drink away from getting belligerent. She hoped he wouldn't get them kicked out of the house.

CHAPTER TWENTY-ONE

Liam wanted to go into the sitting room, where Steve and Jason were talking. There might be an opportunity to talk to Jason alone if Steve had to use the toilet. But when he got up, Doreen told him sharply to stay where he was.

Perhaps she knew what he was thinking.

He hoped Caroline heeded his note.

What a Valentine's Day.

Liam would have loved to talk to Emily, but his phone had no signal. Should he have continued on to Emily's house earlier?

Overthinking plagued him, but he couldn't stop doing it.

Should he feel guilty for involving Caroline and Jason? He didn't want to put them in danger, but he had to save his own skin. He needed a way out.

Doreen looked up from her newspaper.

She said, "That girl doesn't love you. Don't kid yourself."

Liam bristled. He hated to hear Doreen talk about Emily. It was as if she sullied his girlfriend just by mentioning her.

"You don't know Emily."

"I know you," Doreen said. "Honestly, no one likes a loser."

She turned back to her newspaper.

Liam wanted to shout at her, but he didn't.

Be patient. Tonight everything will end.

Liam had no idea what his life would look like the next day, but he was sure it would be completely different. And it couldn't be any worse. He only needed to survive the coming hours.

It sounded like Steve was doing a good job of getting Jason roaring drunk. Their voices echoed down the hall from the sitting room. Jason was slurring his words, but Steve had a constitution that Hunter S. Thompson would have envied.

All Liam's hopes rested in Caroline alone.

CHAPTER TWENTY-TWO

Caroline had no idea when she fell asleep but, at some stage, she must have, because she woke when Jason staggered into the room. He pushed the door open too hard, smashing it into the wall behind.

"Caroline? I love you," Jason slurred.

Caroline's head was foggy with sleep. Jason turned on the ceiling light and staggered over to the bed. Caroline shielded her eyes.

"Would you turn that off?"

"I'm sorry, but I love you. I love you, Caroline. I'm saying it."

"Be quiet. Would you close the door?"

Jason laughed. "I love the way you close doors, Caroline. I love—"

"Shush. You can love me tomorrow."

Jason pushed the door shut. "Caroline, I love the way you shush me. No one could shush me the way you do."

"You're so drunk."

"Are you wearing the panties, Caroline?"

"What? That was you?" Caroline sat up in the bed. "I nearly blamed Liam."

Jason burst out laughing. "It's Valentine's Day."

"Oh my god. Are you coming to bed?"

Jason shrugged. "I don't know. I'd like to stay up, but we drank all the whiskey. I drank most of it, actually."

"I can smell it from here." Caroline turned on the bedside lamp. "Come and lie down."

Jason turned off the ceiling light and staggered over. He threw himself on the mattress next to her. The frame groaned beneath him.

"For god's sake, don't break the bed," Caroline told him.

"Don't worry. They're fine people. Steve is a fine guy. He didn't mind me drinking his whiskey to the last drop. A real gent."

Now that she was awake, Caroline realised she needed to use the bathroom. She swung her legs over the side of the bed. The floor was cool under her bare feet.

Jason blinked in surprise. "Where are you going?"

"I'll be back in a second."

"See if you can find some whiskey."

"You've had more than enough. You'll feel rotten in the morning."

Caroline walked out of the room to the sound of Jason's drunken laughter. The house was quiet. She had no idea of the time. Before midnight anyway, as her alarm had not yet sounded.

She crept to the bathroom, moving as silently as she could, though she was sure that Steve and Doreen were not yet in bed. Surely, they wouldn't turn in for the night before Jason.

The lacy underwear sat where she'd left them. Caroline stuffed them in the bin, then used the toilet, washed her hands and stepped into the hallway again.

The house was still.

Caroline walked up the hall. She stopped outside Frank's room, the room she was meant to steer clear of.

He's very private. Very particular about his personal space.

That was what Doreen had said.

A thought struck Caroline. What if Frank was in the house? What if he was in his room right now? Caroline's skin prickled. Could she feel the presence of another person nearby? Or was her imagination playing tricks on her?

There was no light under the door.

But a red stain was visible on the floor.

Caroline crouched down. Some red liquid seemed to have dried on the floor just under the door. Her first thought was—

"Can I help you?"

"Shit." Caroline jumped.

Doreen stood in the doorway to the kitchen. "What are you doing?"

Her tone was like that of Caroline's old geography teacher, who liked to ask the class questions she already knew the answers to.

"I... I thought I heard something in that room."

"Impossible. Frank isn't here."

Doreen began to walk down the hall as Caroline got to her feet.

Caroline glanced at the floor. "Yes. Of course. It must have been the wind."

Suddenly, it seemed important to get back to her bedroom. Doreen took a step down the hall. Caroline took a step up it. Her heart was racing. The spare bedroom lay halfway between them.

Doreen said, "I told you to leave Frank's room alone."

Caroline was nearly at the door.

So was Doreen.

"Yes, sorry. It was the wind. The sound I heard. Good night."

Caroline grabbed the handle and scrambled into the bedroom. Slamming the door, she pressed her back against it until she heard Doreen walking away.

CHAPTER TWENTY-THREE

Doreen stepped into the kitchen and closed the door behind her. She paused there and shook her head.

"What is it?" Liam said, his voice low. He wasn't sure he wanted to know the answer.

Doreen walked to the door leading to the other hall.

"Come with me," she said.

Liam got to his feet. Slowly he followed his mother down the corridor. Doreen ducked her head into the sitting room and spoke to Steve in a low voice. Then she made for the laundry room.

Liam followed.

What was this about?

As soon as he stepped inside the laundry room, Doreen backhanded him across the face.

"What did you say to that girl?"

She hit him again, but not before he got his hands up. He managed to block the blow.

"What did you tell her?"

"Nothing!"

"Don't lie to me."

"I'm not."

"I bet you told her lies about us."

Liam turned to run but Steve was right behind him. He smashed his fist into Liam's throat.

Gasping for breath, Liam dropped to his knees.

"Tie him up," Doreen said, handing Steve a length of thick hemp rope. She prised Liam's jaws apart and stuffed another piece of rope between his teeth, while Steve bound his hands behind his back.

"Where should we put him?"

Doreen pointed to the wall next to the washing machine. The farthest place from the door. Steve dragged Liam there and shoved him down, so Liam was sitting on the concrete floor with his back against the wall. Both the wall and the floor were freezing cold.

Doreen came and stood in front of him.

"You just killed that girl. You might as well have slit her throat yourself. Her boyfriend too."

Liam's eyes went wide. He tried to shout, but he could only grunt.

"Are you happy with yourself? You killed them both. I told you to keep your loser mouth shut, and you couldn't even do that. You want to get us in trouble?"

Liam tried to speak again, but it was useless. Tears streamed down his face.

"What do you think we should do with him?" Steve asked.

"We'll have plenty of time to think of that once our guests have been dealt with."

"Right you are."

Steve kissed Doreen on the lips. They killed the light when they went out, leaving Liam in the dark.

CHAPTER TWENTY-FOUR

Caroline lay in bed in the darkness. Next to her, Jason, still fully clothed, snored loudly. Caroline's stomach churned, unnerved after her encounter with Doreen.

An hour later, she still couldn't settle. It was hard to pinpoint why she was so anxious. Doreen hadn't threatened her. But she picked up a weird vibe.

Caroline thought of Frank's room. Was the stain on the floor blood? That was what Caroline had been wondering when Doreen surprised her. And, if it was, what did that mean?

A rumbling sound came from outside.

Caroline strained to hear, but that was difficult with Jason's snoring. She gave him a punch on the arm.

He groaned. Slowly, his eyes opened.

"What was that for?"

"Listen," Caroline said. She flicked on the bedside lamp.

Jason rubbed his eyes. "I don't hear anything."

"It sounded like... like an engine."

"Huh?"

"Maybe a car or van."

Jason sighed and sat up. His eyelids were heavy. "We're a long way from the road."

"Not on the road. It was right outside."

"I doubt it."

Caroline said, "Seriously. I think they're doing something out there."

"Like what?"

Caroline had no idea. She checked the time on her phone. 23:45. Her midnight rendezvous was meant to happen in fifteen minutes.

She turned off her alarm. There was no need for it now.

Was the sound made by Liam? What could he possibly be doing?

"I'm going to take a look outside," Caroline said.

"What?"

"You stay here."

Jason wiped the sleep out of his eyes. He swung his legs over the side of the bed. "No, I'll go."

"I'm not helpless. I'm perfectly capable—"

"It's not that. I want to have a smoke," Jason said.

"Be careful."

Jason chuckled, stretching his arms out, and rubbing his eyes again. "I'm not going far."

"I don't like this."

Jason leaned over and kissed Caroline's cheek. "I'll have a quick cigarette and see what's happening. Alright?"

Caroline nodded. She watched Jason stagger out of the bedroom.

Outside, the engine noise had stopped.

Everything was silent.

CHAPTER TWENTY-FIVE

Jason flicked on the kitchen light and looked around for his jacket, but he couldn't see it anywhere. Before he went to bed, Doreen had said that his clothes had been washed, and were in the dryer, so they'd be ready to wear first thing in the morning. Maybe she'd put his muddy jacket in the wash too.

The cold air might be nice, Jason decided. He knew he was very drunk, and the sensation was no longer pleasant.

He opened the door and stepped outside. Slushy snow splashed under his feet. Shivering, he fished a cigarette out of the packet in his jeans and lit it. Caroline must have imagined the engine. Jason couldn't hear anything like that. Nevertheless, he walked around the side of the house.

A blazing light caught his attention as he rounded the corner. The garage doors were wide open, revealing the huge interior. The first thing he saw was a gleaming black SUV. It looked like the one he and Caroline had encountered on the road.

The one that nearly killed them.

Caroline's Peugeot stood next to it. Its back wheels rested on the ground. The front wheels were hoisted up, attached to a white tow truck.

The cigarette fell out of Jason's mouth.

Steve had said he wouldn't be able to tow their car off the road tonight. Doreen had said that too. But here it was.

Jason wondered what else Doreen and Steve might have lied about. He thought of Steve's injury, and Liam's face – pale and scared the whole evening.

"Take him now."

Jason spun towards the voice, as a wrench smashed into the side of his skull with a sickening crunch of bone. He dropped to his hands and knees.

Steve and Doreen stood over him.

"Again," Doreen said.

Jason looked up. "No. Wait—"

Another blow, and everything went black.

CHAPTER TWENTY-SIX

The laundry room had a small window above the washing machine. It let a little light in, but the room was still dark. In that darkness, Liam struggled to free his hands.

The rough rope binding his wrists together dug into his skin. But he struggled on, trying to work his way free. He thought he was beginning to make progress when the door opened.

He froze as the light came on.

Steve stepped into the room, dragging Jason by the legs.

He was unconscious.

Or worse.

Liam groaned. He tried to speak but the rope in his mouth stopped him.

Breathing hard with the exertion, Steve pulled Jason across the floor. Jason's face scraped against the concrete.

Doreen stepped into the room and put her hands on her hips.

"This is all your fault," she said.

Steve let go of Jason, dropping him in the corner of the room, face-down.

"Shit. He was heavy for such a skinny guy," Steve said. Panting, he straightened up. "I really feel like a whiskey. Wish I hadn't let that bastard drink it all."

Doreen said, "Let's have a smoke. Then we can take care of the other one."

Steve nodded and followed Doreen out the door.

Before the door closed, Doreen stuck her head back in.

"I hope you're happy with yourself," she sneered. "You killed three people today. You just sit here and think about that."

The door shut and the light flicked off.

CHAPTER TWENTY-SEVEN

The longer Caroline waited for Jason to come back to bed, the more fearful she became. She sat up, nightmarish scenarios running through her mind. A few minutes ago, she'd thought she heard voices. Perhaps it was the wind, though. Or Jason, who was drunk. He might have been talking to himself while he smoked yet another cigarette.

Caroline's phone said it was midnight. Time for her to meet Liam. Had Jason run into him already?

She stepped out of the bed, found her shoes and opened the door to the corridor. Lights out, doors closed. No sign of anyone. She continued to the kitchen. The light was on, but there was no sign of anyone.

Caroline found the back door unlocked.

She stepped outside.

Feeling sick with fright, she walked alongside the building, passing the window to the spare bedroom, then the window to Frank's room.

She stopped and stepped on the tips of her toes, so she could look inside the window. On the other side of the glass, the curtains were closed, but there was a gap of about an inch where they didn't meet.

Caroline could make out a shape on the floor, but she wasn't sure what it was. The room was so dark. She waited for her vision to adjust to the darkness. Slowly the shape came into focus.

A body lay at the foot of the bed. It was covered by a blanket, but the shape was distinct.

Caroline felt a pulse of horror. Was that Frank?

Behind her, the kitchen door opened.

Caroline ran to the corner and flung herself around it. She was outside the bathroom now, and out of sight of Doreen and Steve, but she heard them talking. They seemed to be standing outside the kitchen door.

Caroline closed her eyes and tried to regain control of herself. Her chest rose and fell, her breathing panicked.

They must have killed him.

Their own son.

That explained why they didn't want her going into his room – and why they'd seemed so wary when she and Jason arrived. They were afraid of their secret getting out. If they'd do such a thing, they'd also kill Caroline and Jason to stop them talking.

Where *was* Jason?

She took a deep breath and ran in the opposite direction to Doreen and Steve. Coming to the garage, she caught sight of the black SUV that had nearly hit her.

Then she saw her Peugeot.

Caroline sprinted to the garage. She might be able to get away by car. The Peugeot was useless, of course. Steve must have brought it here on the tow truck, but presumably the car had not been repaired yet. She noticed a machine standing next to the Peugeot. A wet vacuum cleaner. What the hell did Steve plan to do with that?

Never mind, Caroline told herself.

The Range Rover was her ticket out of here. She ran over to it and tried its doors, but they were locked. The key fob must be in the house, or in Steve's pocket.

The tow truck was locked too.

"Okay," Caroline whispered.

New plan.

She needed to find the keys to one of the cars, and she needed to find Jason. Once she did that, the two of them could get away from this place.

She remembered passing a laundry room when they entered the house earlier. There had been a key rack on the wall.

She ran along the side of the house until she found the right window. She got on the tips of her toes and peered inside.

Liam was tied up on the floor.

Beside him, Jason lay still on the floor.

The sight of this new horror did not make Caroline back away. It made her more determined to get inside. She had to find out if Jason was alright.

She dragged a flower box over to the window and stepped up onto it. With her elbow, she smashed the window, hoping the sound would not carry on the wind. The blow hurt, but she ignored the pain.

She pulled herself up onto the narrow windowsill and jumped down into the room.

CHAPTER TWENTY-EIGHT

The breaking glass startled Liam. He craned his neck to the side so he could see the window. Caroline climbed through. She dropped to the floor, crossed the room and fumbled around for the light switch. The room lit up.

She went to Jason, dropping on her knees next to him.

"Jason?"

She shook his body. No response. Nothing. Liam saw the look on Caroline's face. Her boyfriend was dead – and it was Liam's fault.

She took a moment, then came over to Liam and hunkered down in front of him. The rough rope was wedged tight in his mouth. She worked it out slowly. When she was done, Liam gasped for breath.

"Tell me what's going on," Caroline said.

Liam looked at the door to the hall.

"They might have heard the glass break."

"Then you better speak quickly."

"Okay."

She untied his hands while he filled her in.

It had started before lunch, when Frank found the Valentine's Day card that Liam had made for Emily.

Somehow Liam had kept his relationship with her a secret for three months. He didn't want his family to know. But Frank had sensed that *something* was up. He searched Liam's room and found the card with a poem Liam had written for her.

Of course, Frank read it aloud to Steve and Doreen while they ate lunch. And the three of them laughed at it.

Frank refused to give the card back. He took it to his room, and Liam followed.

"Emily Brown?" Frank said, smiling at the thought. "You and Emily Brown?"

The three of them went to the same school, and it irritated Liam that Frank knew who she was. Normally Liam stifled his habitual feelings. Rage. Fear. Self-loathing. Why not? Doreen and Steve always made sure that Liam knew he was a loser.

He'd become accustomed to their cruelty, had accepted it as normal – at least, until Emily told him, *Some people shouldn't be allowed to be parents.*

Doreen hated the fact that she herself was a twin. She was delighted when Frank came along. He was the perfect little son she'd always wanted. Not so happy when Liam followed nine minutes later. An unwanted freebie. Identical, but not the same.

When Liam followed Frank to his room, adrenaline was pulsing through his body. He wasn't sure he could control his feelings.

"Are you going to give her your card now?" Frank asked.

"None of your business."

"What if I meet her instead?" Frank grinned. "I bet she'll never know the difference."

Liam's anger began spin out of control. He welcomed the feeling. He wanted to hurt Frank, wanted Frank to be the one who suffered, for once. Frank held the card high in the air and teased Liam like he was a kid.

Liam lost it then.

His first punch hit Frank in the side, below the ribs. It made Frank double over, dropping the card on the floor.

"You're dead," Frank said. His voice was icy, and Liam realised it was no figure of speech.

Liam tried to leave the room, but Frank grabbed him from behind. They struggled and fell into the mirrored door of Frank's wardrobe. The mirror shattered, falling to the floor around them in jagged shards.

Liam scrambled to his feet, but Frank was faster. He pulled the lace out of his shoe, wrapped it around Liam's neck and began to strangle him with it.

"I'm going to go and meet Emily. I'm going to have a real good time with her," Frank whispered in his ear.

Liam smashed the back of his head into Frank's nose. The impact made a horrible crunch. Frank dropped the lace.

"You're so fucking dead," Frank shouted.

Liam tried to crawl away across the carpeted floor, but Frank grabbed his leg and flipped him onto his back. Frank sat on Liam's chest, driving the air out of him, and pulled a switchblade out of his jeans.

"Get off me," Liam said.

"Shut up."

Many times, Frank had threatened him with this blade. Many more times, he had stabbed him with it, or cut him with it. Small wounds, Liam supposed, but they all added up.

The sight of a knife now made Liam frantic. Frank's eyes were wild as he pressed the button on the knife and the blade shot out.

"No," Liam said.

"Shut up."

Liam reached out for something, anything, on the floor. His fingers touched a long shard from the mirror. His only hope.

Frank was drawing back his arm, preparing to stab the knife into Liam's neck.

Liam had no choice.

He grabbed the piece of broken mirror and thrust it as hard as he could into Frank's side. It went in deep

Frank looked down at the wound in surprise. Liam pulled out the shard and stabbed it into Frank again. The knife fell from Frank's hand. He gasped, then keeled over.

That was when Doreen and Steve tore into the room.

"What have you done?" Doreen screamed.

Liam backed away. He'd killed the one they loved. There was no telling what would happen now.

Steve hurried over to Frank, who was taking his last breath. He cradled him in his arms. Doreen got on her knees and touched Frank's face, but the life was already draining out of it.

Liam ran out the door.

He took Steve's Range Rover and drove off with the vague idea of going to Emily's house and asking her to elope. Along the way, he realised what a stupid idea it was. But if he didn't do that, what could he do? Where could he go?

Nowhere.

Eventually, he turned around and started driving home. That was when he came across Caroline and Jason at the petrol station. All he knew was he needed help. If he went home alone, he thought Doreen and Steve would kill him.

So he sabotaged the Peugeot. Nothing to feel guilty about. He figured a wet vac would get the gravel out later and make the engine run again.

Caroline and Jason were heading in the direction of the McGlynn house anyway. It was the only house around, so if their car broke down nearby, they'd probably come to the McGlynns looking for help.

He panicked when he met them on the road. Of course, he should have picked them up and brought them to the house himself, but he drove straight past.

When Liam got home, Steve had come after him. Liam smashed Steve in the face with a torch. Then he'd gone down the cliff road looking for Barney. When he came back to the house, Caroline and Jason had arrived.

And by then everything was hurtling towards disaster.

CHAPTER TWENTY-NINE

Liam spoke quickly, avoiding eye contact as he did so. When he stopped, Caroline sensed that there was much more he wanted to say. He had only given her the briefest account of what happened, but that would have to be enough for now.

"I'm so sorry," Liam said, looking up for the first time. "I didn't want to cause you trouble. I just needed help. I didn't know what to do."

"You should have reported the accident."

Liam nodded. "I should have but I didn't. They think I told you what happened."

"What if you did tell me? Why are they so worried about that?"

Liam shrugged. "I guess they're afraid of what I might say – about how they treated me over the years. They aren't nice people," he added.

"I don't understand why they let us in at all," Caroline said.

"It would have looked suspicious if they turned you away. And maybe they wondered if you already knew something."

Caroline thought she should have felt colder towards Liam. But he hadn't killed Jason. Doreen and Steve had. And what happened with Frank? It was almost understandable. She squeezed his shoulder.

"Let's get out of here." She helped him to his feet and they walked over to the key rack. "Are the key fobs for the cars here?"

Liam shook his head. "Steve has them."

Caroline heard footsteps in the hall. Moving fast. "They're coming."

"Go out the window."

Liam boosted Caroline. She crawled through the window, out into the night. The lights of the garage still blazed. She turned and held out a hand to Liam as he crawled through the window after her.

Behind him, the door burst open.

Steve saw them and ran across the room. He grabbed at Liam's foot, but Liam kicked out hard, smashing his runner into Steve's face. Steve fell on his ass. Caroline pulled Liam as he scrambled out the window.

"You're going to pay," Doreen screamed. "You ungrateful little shit."

Liam dropped to the ground next to Caroline. If it was possible, his face had turned a shade paler.

He's only seventeen, Caroline reminded herself. *And that's his mother.*

A chill, which had nothing to do with the cold, passed through her.

"Come on," she said, and set off running for the garage, holding her loose jeans up with one hand. She wished she had a jacket, but there was nothing she could do about that.

"We can't take a car."

"I don't want those fuckers to be able to take one either."

She ran through the open doorway. Tools hung on hooks on one wall. Every kind imaginable. Too many.

"I need something sharp," Caroline said.

Liam pulled a chisel off the wall and handed it to her. He took another one himself, and ran to the SUV, where he burst two of the tyres.

Caroline burst two of the tow truck's tyres.

Voices nearby.

"Let's go," Caroline called. They threw down the tools and ran outside. Steve and Doreen were jogging towards them from the house. Caroline was in good shape. Liam looked like he was too. They would be able to outrun the older couple.

Caroline hurried across the driveway, towards the yew tree and the road that led away from the house. They needed to keep running.

And then?

Caroline didn't know.

Behind her, Liam called out. She turned to see that he had tripped. Doreen and Steve were closing in on him.

Steve held a wrench in his hand, and he looked like he meant to use it.

CHAPTER THIRTY

Caroline didn't want to lose any time, but she forced herself to run back where Liam had fallen. She took his hand and helped him to his feet as Steve reached them.

Teeth clenched, he swung the wrench at Liam's head, missing by an inch. Then they were running again, Caroline still holding her jeans up, so she didn't trip too.

"Are you okay?" Caroline said.

"Yeah. Just run," Liam shouted.

She headed towards the road.

"Not that way," he said. "To the cliff."

"Are you crazy?"

"Trust me."

"I don't want to die."

"Neither do I."

Liam ran in a wide curve around Steve and Doreen.

Reluctantly, Caroline followed.

They passed the house and turned down a mud trail that ran along the cliff face. The Atlantic Ocean roared. A terrifying drop, only six feet away, on their left side. Caroline followed in Liam's footsteps, jogging now rather than running, to reduce the risk of tripping. No point getting away from Doreen and Steve if she was going to let her own panic get her killed.

She could barely think. Knowing that there was such a huge drop right beside her? That short-circuited her brain. Dizzy as it made her, she kept going.

The cliff face was uneven, and the path roughly followed its contours, generally remaining about six feet from the precipice. On the other side, the ground sloped upwards.

"We're nearly there," Liam shouted over his shoulder.

"Nearly where?"

Liam pointed ahead. A picnic table stood in the grass at the side of the path, about twenty feet from the cliff edge.

"Steve put it there years ago. It's his favourite place to smoke."

Great, Caroline thought.

"The weather was good yesterday," Liam said.

"So what?" Caroline shouted, wondering if he was demented.

"So I was cycling. I left my bike there."

Sure enough, a mountain bike was chained to the table. Caroline doubted that the chain was there to prevent theft. Perhaps it was to secure the bike against the ferocious wind. As she drew closer, she saw that the picnic table too was secured. Each leg was encased in cement, which in turn was attached to a rocky outcrop. She figured that was why it hadn't flown into the sea during a storm.

Liam unlocked the bike and ran with it back to the path. Caroline followed.

"Get on," he said.

"Are you kidding me?"

"If we can make it to the end of this path, we'll come out on the road you were driving on earlier. This is a shortcut."

Caroline shook her head.

In the distance, she heard the roar of an engine.

"That can't be a car..." she said.

The path was too narrow. A car would never make it down here. And anyway, they had burst the tyres.

Liam shrugged. "Maybe they didn't notice the tyres. Or maybe they don't care. They're crazy. They'll do anything to get me." He swung his leg over the saddle and looked back at her. "Are you coming?"

She got on behind him and wrapped her arms around his waist. He kicked off and began pedalling furiously. At first the bike wobbled from side to side. Caroline unleashed a stream of curses and closed her eyes, but she found that was even scarier, so she opened them again.

The cliff was so close... but the ground to the right looked too rough to cycle on. An obstacle course of rock and grass. They had to stick to the path.

The sound of the engine grew louder and headlights swept over them. Caroline squeezed Liam tighter.

"They're coming! Pedal faster."

His legs worked frantically. Caroline struggled to hold on as the bike bumped along. She could hear waves crashing at the foot of the cliff. Ahead, the ground rose in a hill.

Caroline risked a glance behind her. The Range Rover was shooting towards them. The vehicle was a crazy angle, with its left wheels on the path, and its right wheels up on the sloping ground next to the path.

It was extremely close. Its deflated front tyres slapped against the ground.

Doreen was sitting in the passenger seat, her trout-like face dark. Behind the wheel, Steve's face was twisted with rage.

The Range Rover was closing the gap.

It was nearly upon them.

"Faster," Caroline screamed in Liam's ear.

He huffed and puffed as they rose the hill ahead. Despite his efforts, they were moving slower and slower. They'd never get away.

"Hold on," Liam shouted as they approached the crest of the hill.

"What?"

The Range Rover came so close that Caroline thought she could feel the heat from the engine.

It was moving so fast. Soon it would crush them.

"Hold on!" Liam shouted.

They reached the top of the hill. On the other side, the path turned right, following the contour of the cliff. Liam wrenched the handlebars to the side. Both Liam and Caroline tumbled to the ground, hitting it hard on their left side. The bike fell on top of them, stabbing Caroline in the ribs.

She gasped.

They rolled onto the grass.

Caroline only saw Doreen and Steve for a second as the Range Rover crested the hill. Steve was wrestling with the wheel, but it was too late. They were moving too fast and the ruined tyres made it impossible for them to correct their course in time.

The Range Rover launched into the air.

Its back wheels landed on the ground, but the front ones were spinning in space. Tipping forward.

The Range Rover tumbled over the side of the cliff and careened out of sight, into the darkness of the ocean.

CHAPTER THIRTY-ONE

It took forty minutes to cycle to the nearest town, if you could call it a town. Nothing more than a cluster of a few dozen houses, one pub, one shop, and a closed-down post office. All together along one road.

It was after 1:00 and everything was closed, but Liam rang the doorbell of a neat little house with a garden full of daffodils.

"We'll do this right," Caroline said. "Okay?"

"Okay," Liam said. He rang the bell a few more times. Emily and her parents would be asleep.

For a while after Doreen and Steve plunged to their deaths, Caroline and Liam sat on the freezing ground, looking out to sea. Liam cried. Caroline couldn't imagine what he felt. Her own feelings were enough of a jumble for her to try and sort out. Horror at the day's events, grief over Jason's death, disbelief at the cruelty of which people were capable, and, now, relief at their escape.

Liam wiped his eyes. He said, "They'll arrest me for what happened to Frank. I should disappear and never come back. I don't want to go to jail."

Caroline shook her head.

"You're young. What happened with Frank was an accident. Don't ruin your life by making the wrong choice now. Do you want to run forever? Do you think Emily would want that?"

There was a long silence while Liam thought.

"I don't know," he said finally.

"Trust that things will turn out alright."

"I don't trust anyone."

"Not even me?" Caroline said.

He shrugged. "Maybe a little."

"Then trust me when I say, I won't leave you alone. Whatever happens next."

"You don't need to babysit me. You're not my Mum."

"I know. Thank fuck for that, right?"

Liam cracked a smile. "Yeah."

"After what we've been through, I reckon you could say we're friends."

They shook hands in the dark.

"Yeah," Liam said again. "Okay."

"Good. Tell the truth. Unburden yourself once and for all. Then you can start thinking about a new life. You might need therapy," Caroline added with a smile.

Liam blew his nose. "I guess so. I'm pretty messed up."

"You're not the only one."

Neither of them had their phone and Liam said he didn't want to go back to the house, didn't want to spend another minute in that place.

So they'd continued down the track, pushing the bike, until they came out on the road. Then they mounted the bike and cycled to Emily's house.

After seven rings of the doorbell, her father opened the door in his dressing gown.

"What on earth is going on?"

"I'm sorry to wake you, but we need to use your phone," Caroline said.

The man turned on the porch light and looked at their faces.

"What's this about?"

Caroline said, "It's an emergency."

A teenage girl in fluffy pink pyjamas appeared behind the man. She had the kindest brown eyes Caroline had seen in a long time. She hurried past her father and threw her arms around Liam.

"Are you okay?" she said. "What happened?"

"It's a long story."

Caroline realised they must look awful. Covered in mud and blood. Clothes ruined. A trail of destruction behind them.

She and Liam *were* friends now. They had gone through hell together, and they had come out the other side.

Caroline smiled. "You must be Emily."

The girl nodded.

"How did you know?"

Caroline didn't reply. She hoped Liam remembered the poem he had written for this girl, because she looked like someone who'd appreciate it. And that was worth more than he probably knew.

ABOUT THE AUTHOR

Alan Gorevan is an award-winning writer and intellectual property attorney. He lives in Dublin, Ireland.

Visit www.alangorevan.com to learn more.

Printed in Great Britain
by Amazon

52943012R00069